Ever seen a jackalope?
Probably not, because they're gone. Extinct.

Like dinosaurs and go-go boots.

Ever wonder what happened
to them? I know, because two
silly sisters told me. They said it
was the absolute truth.

So put on your listening ears, zip your lips, and get ready for

Jackalope

WRITTEN BY
**Janet Stevens &
Susan Stevens Crummel**

ILLUSTRATED BY
Janet Stevens

Harcourt, Inc.
San Diego   New York   London
Printed in Singapore

Gather around, come sit on the ground,
And I'll tell you a tale of a hare.
And all of it's true, as best I recall,
Except for some parts here and there.
The branches are full on the Jack family tree
With jackrabbits famous and not.
There's Jack and the beanstalk and Jack-in-the-box.
Folks talk of those two a lot.
But one branch is empty, and all that is left
Is a sign that hangs down by a rope.
A sign with the name of the Jack who is gone.
All it says is one word:
JACKALOPE.

Once upon a time, in the land of cactus and cattle, there lived a very unhappy jackrabbit.

"I hate being ordinary. Nobody notices me. Nobody runs away from me. Nobody is afraid of me. I can be fierce, too, can't I? I'll ask Mirror—he always tells the truth. Hey, Mirror, look at this!" Jackrabbit froze in his scariest pose. "Mirror, Mirror, cracked and small, who's the fiercest one of all?" He waited for a reply.

"At the risk of being rude—I think Longhorn's one mean dude."

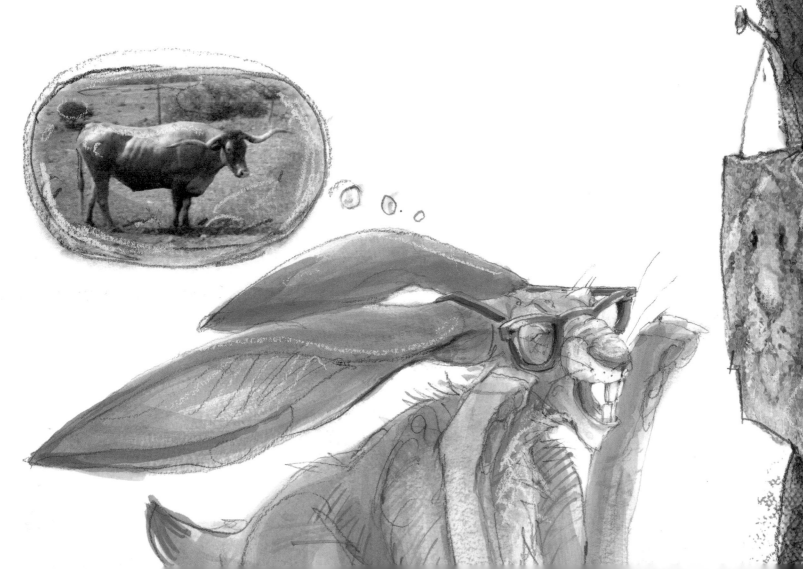

"Longhorn? That overgrown piece of beef jerky? I can be scarier than he is. Look at this!" Jack twisted his ears sideways, snorted, and pawed at the ground like Longhorn. "Mirror, Mirror, on the tree, who's the scariest? Say it's me!"

"Heed my words, for they are true. Horned Toad's scarier than you!"

"Horned Toad? That stubby little pancake? I can be more ferocious than she is. Look at this!" Jack rolled in some mud and shaped his fur into spikes like Horned Toad. "Mirror, Mirror, hanging there, say that I'm one scary hare!"

"Jack, you only make me smile. Give it up—it's not your style."

Jackrabbit grabbed Mirror off the tree. "Mirror, Mirror, piece of glass, here you go—in the grass!" He tossed Mirror on the ground and walked off.

Jack saw a lone star in the evening sky. "Star-light, star-bright, first star I see tonight. Listen up, hear my plea, make me anything but me! And while you're at it, Star, I'd like some fangs…and claws…maybe a stinger…a big, sharp beak…and pointy horns—real ones." He curled up, closed his eyes, and tried to sleep.

Jack wasn't happy just being himself.
He had to be scary and feared.
He wished and he hoped and he tossed and he turned.
At dawn a strange creature appeared.

Someone poked Jack in the ribs. "Having a bad *hare* day?"

"Who are you?"

"I'm your fairy godrabbit! You wished on a star, and that's where I come in. See this star on my wand? Star wishes are the only ones I can grant. I don't do wishbones, wishing wells, birthday candles, and all that other stuff. Now *lettuce* see, you wished for fangs, claws, a stinger, beak, and horns. Sorry, there's a one-wish limit."

Jackrabbit shook his head. "I want them all. I can't choose."

"I know what I'd wish for. Some normal clothes!"
Fairy Godrabbit rolled her eyes. "Look at me. I look
like a tossed salad. Dressing in this getup is for the
birds! I wish…"

"Is this your wish or my wish?" Jack interrupted.

"Okay, okay. I see you don't *carrot* all about me!
So choose!"

Jack paused. "I want… I want… horns!"

"Horns?" Fairy Godrabbit moaned. "Why did it have
to be horns? I've turned pumpkins into carriages, frogs
into princes, and rags into gowns, but I've never done
horns. I'll have to look this up. Luckily, I brought
my new unabridged, fully illustrated, first-time-in-
paperback, step-by-step copy of *Wishes for Wabbits.*"

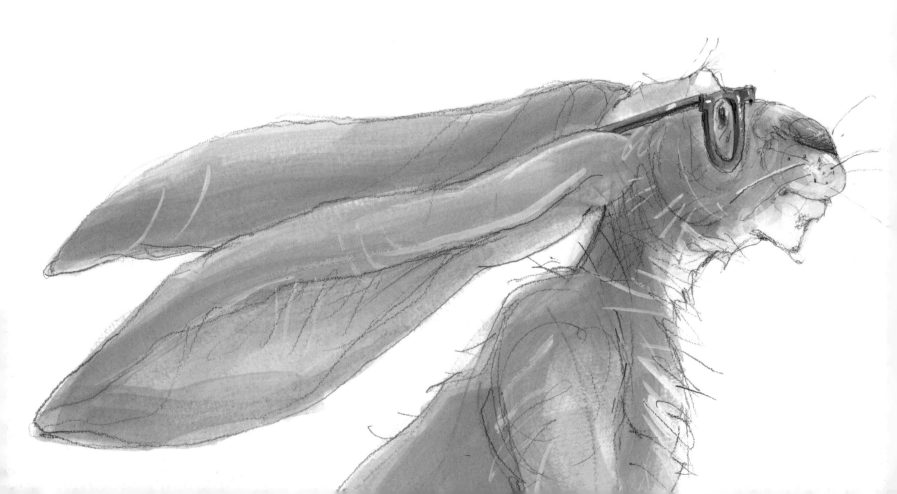

Fairy Godrabbit flipped through the pages. "Hmmm. 'Chapter Eight: Wishes Beginning with H. Hair (longer, shorter)'—no. 'High heels (glass, ruby)'—no. Oh, here it is. 'Horns (trumpets, trombones)'—now *that'll* look cute on your head. I think you mean *these:* 'Horns (like antlers).' Ready, Jack?" She waved her wand. "Wait, it says there's one condition: Never tell a lie or—or else—"

"Just hurry up," snapped Jack.

"Magic dust, do your stuff.
Make this hare mean and tough.
Pointy horns are his hope.
Make them like ... like ... Antelope!"

Poof!

When the magic dust had settled, there
stood Jackrabbit with horns like an antelope.
You just might call him a jackalope.

He pranced. He strutted. He puffed out his chest.
His horns were a sight to behold!
At last he was scary. At last he was fierce.
But Jackalope had to be told.

"Mirror, Mirror, on the ground,
who's the scariest one around?"
There was no reply.
"Who needs that silly old
mirror, anyway? I know I'm the
scariest one of all." Jackalope
left Mirror in the grass and
headed down the path to find
Hummingbird.

"Hey, Hummingbird, look at me!" Jackalope froze in his scariest pose.

"Jack! Where did you get those horns?"

"They're mine and I've always had them," Jackalope boasted.

"Jumpin' jackrabbits, those horns *grew* right before my very own eyes!" Hummingbird zoomed away and almost flew smack-dab into Squirrel.

"Hey, Squirrel, look at me!" Jackalope froze in his scariest pose.

"Jack! Where did you get those horns?"

"They're mine and I've always had them," Jackalope boasted.

"Leapin' lizards, those are *growin'* horns. I'm out of here!" Squirrel hightailed it down the path.

Jackalope teetered from the weight on his head. "Being scary is hard work," he said to himself.

But Jackalope was not alone.

Two eyes were watching and two ears were listening
And one mouth was watering, too.
Coyote was tired of acorns and berries—
He wanted some jackrabbit stew.

"Well, look at you," said Coyote. Jackalope turned.

"Are those horns I see?" Coyote stepped closer. "How extraordinary! I really can't see them from so far away. I need a better look." He stepped even closer. "Well, I'll be. Can I touch them?" He reached out . . .

. . . and jumped at Jackalope!

The chasing began and the two of them ran
Up and down, in and out, all around.
As Jackalope dived for his old hiding place,
His huge horns got stuck in the ground.

"Help!" Jackalope struggled.

"Well, isn't this handy?" Coyote snickered. "Dinner waiting to be cooked—a jackrabbit kabob. I'll just build a fire right under him. He's not going anywhere!" Coyote wandered off to look for firewood.

"I'm stuck! Why did I wish for these horns?" Jackalope cried. "Fairy Godrabbit, come back!"

"Okay, you don't have to yell—I'm right here! My, my, look at those horns. Just how many lies have you told?"

"Lies? I haven't told any lies," Jack replied.

"Okay, maybe a few. Now, how do you get rid of these horns?"

"*Beets* me!" Fairy Godrabbit shook her head. "You get one wish. You wanted horns, you got horns."

"But surely you can undo a wish. Hurry! Look it up!" Jackalope pleaded. "Coyote's coming back and he's gonna roast me like a hot dog, gobble me up whole, and pick his teeth with my horns!"

"Now that's a problem!" Fairy Godrabbit opened her manual. "Here it is. 'Chapter Twenty-seven: Undoing Wishes. Number one: You can't. Number two: If you think you can, see number one.' Oh dear. Tough luck. But maybe I can *move* the horns—you know, transplant them. I'll give it a try.

Magic dust, rescue hare.
Put these horns over—"

"*There* is a nice piece of kindling for my fire!" Coyote grabbed the wand from Fairy Godrabbit. Magic dust sprinkled all over her.

The horns disappeared from Jackalope's head.
He hopped up and dashed out of sight!
But where do you think those horns reappeared?
On Fairy Godrabbit? That's right!

Jack kept running. He bolted up a hill and jumped into a hollow tree.

Coyote shrugged. "*Hare* today, gone tomorrow!" He turned and eyed Fairy Godrabbit. "Dinner ran off, but here's dessert!"

She glared. "You *butternut* come any closer or I'll *squash* you!"

"Yeah, right," laughed Coyote. "I'm gonna toast you like a marshmallow!" He grabbed her by the horns, stuck her in the ground, and went to find more wood.

"Someone help me!" screamed Fairy Godrabbit. "Prince Charming? Knight in shining armor? Ex-Jackalope? I know you're out there. I could use your help! *Please!*"

Way down deep in that dark, hollow tree,
Jack heard her cries of distress.
Should he go save Fairy Godrabbit now?
Or should he stay put? What a mess!

Jack thought fast. "I have to go back!" He struggled out of the tree. His fur was covered with sticky sap. "She helped me, and now she needs me. Hold on, Fairy Godrabbit, I'm coming to the rescue!"

He dashed downhill,

then tripped, rolled, bounced,

and rolled some more.

Everything in his path stuck.
Leaves. Twigs.

Weeds. Dirt. Cactus.

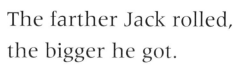

The farther Jack rolled,
the bigger he got.

Meanwhile, Coyote lit a fire under Fairy Godrabbit.

Rustle, rustle…

"What's that?" Coyote wondered.

Rustle, rustle, rustle…

"Who's there?" He looked around.

Rustle, rustle…

"Hey, Coyote—look at me!"

Coyote turned—gasped—then burst out laughing. "A giant bush-rabbit! That's the funniest thing I've ever seen!" He laughed so hard he hee-hawed like a donkey and snorted like a pig.

His laugh became a howl, and he howled so hard he tumbled right downhill and into the stream. Coyote was still howling as he floated away.

Jack pulled Fairy Godrabbit out of the ground and stamped out the fire.

"Oh, Jack, I knew you'd *turnip*! How brave. You really are my knight in shining . . . shining . . . stuff!"

Fairy Godrabbit picked up a charred stick. "My wand! It's burned to a crisp. No more magic dust. No more wishes. And I'm stuck with these horns forever."

"You could decorate them with *hornaments*," Jack chuckled. "Wait a minute! Somewhere in this mess there might be some magic dust left on me."

"On me, too!" cried Fairy Godrabbit.

They shook and twisted, turned and danced. Stuff flew everywhere. Leaves. Twigs. Weeds. Dirt. Cactus. Vegetables. Magic dust.

"Quick, make a wish," said Jack.

Fairy Godrabbit took a deep breath.

"Magic dust, one last time.

Oh, my dear...this won't rhyme.

Just get these horns off me—now!"

Poof!

The horns vanished.

"That's it. My fairy godrabbit days are over. Now I'm just an ordinary hare, so it's back to my ordinary name, Jill." She turned and walked away.

"Wait!" cried Jack. "Stay. We can be ordinary together, like two *peas* in a pod."

Jill paused. "Didn't you want to be scary and fierce?"

"No way. It's hazardous to my health," said Jack. "Ordinary's safer. I'm happy that way. And if you stayed here, I'd be happier, even with your *corny* vegetable talk."

"Oh, how can I believe you?" asked Jill. "Remember *Z-z-z-z-i-p*?"

"Let's ask Mirror," said Jack. "He always tells the truth. Mirror, Mirror, friend so small, who's the happiest one of all?" There was no reply.

"Hello, Mirror, are you there?"

"I don't just reflect, I need your respect."

Jackrabbit picked up the mirror and polished it.

Mirror sparkled. "Who's the happiest? Now it's three: Jack and Jill and Mirror—that's me!"

Hold on—it's not over yet. There's more!

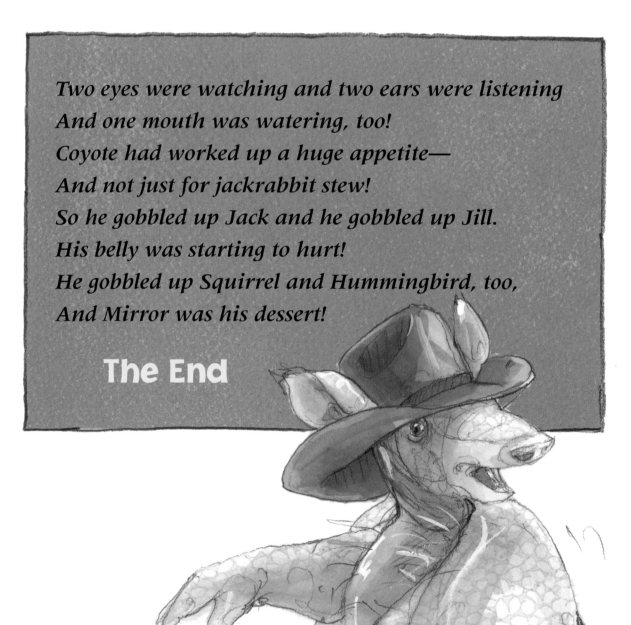

Two eyes were watching and two ears were listening
And one mouth was watering, too!
Coyote had worked up a huge appetite—
And not just for jackrabbit stew!
So he gobbled up Jack and he gobbled up Jill.
His belly was starting to hurt!
He gobbled up Squirrel and Hummingbird, too,
And Mirror was his dessert!

The End

Ha! Just kidding. You didn't believe that, did you?
Don't worry—here's what really happened:

Jackalope's gone, but his legend lives on
As I tell of his tale here and there.
And don't you all mope for that ol' Jackalope,
For he's happy to be just a hare.

Mirror and Jack and their new buddy, Jill,
Were a trio forever, they say.
And if it's real quiet, I know you can hear
That coyote still howling today.

So when you're out gazing at night at the sky
And you happen to see the first star,
Why, don't you be wishing for something you're not—
It's better to be who you are!

The End
(Really.)

Well, that about wraps it up! Hey, speaking of being something you're not, listen to this!

Did you know that a jackrabbit isn't a rabbit? It's a hare! The babies aren't bunnies. They're called leverets, and they're born fully furred, eyes wide open, ready to hop. Jackrabbits outrun their natural enemies (including coyotes) by using their strong hind legs; they need that plain fur for camouflage. Jackrabbits like to eat herbs and shrubs.

The antelope of North America isn't an antelope. It's a pronghorn! It can run faster than most other animals in the world, but it never jumps over a fence. Get this—its horns are unique. They're *not* antlers, but they branch, shed, and grow back like antlers. Nearly half the pronghorn's diet is cactus. Yuck!

And remember that horned toad? It's not a toad. It's a lizard! It's very gentle, but it scares off predators by doing some scary-looking things, like puffing up its body to make it look bigger and squirting blood from its eyes. Whoa! It eats live ants by lassoing them with its long, sticky tongue.

The two silly sisters who told me this story don't eat shrubs, cactus, or ants. They like to graze at all-you-can-eat buffets!

For all our cousins on the Real family tree—even those who convinced us that jackalopes exist

—Janet and Susie

www.HarcourtBooks.com

Library of Congress Cataloging-in-Publication Data
Stevens, Janet.
Jackalope/written by Janet Stevens and Susan Stevens Crummel; illustrated by Janet Stevens.
p. cm.
Summary: A jackrabbit who wishes to be feared asks his fairy godrabbit for horns and becomes the first jackalope, but there's one condition: he must not tell lies.
[1. Jackrabbits—Fiction. 2. Horns—Fiction. 3. Magic—Fiction. 4. Honesty—Fiction.
5. Self-acceptance—Fiction. 6. Desert animals—Fiction. 7. Humorous stories.]
I. Crummel, Susan Stevens. II. Title.
PZ7.S84453Jac 2003
[Fic]—dc21   2002005342
ISBN 0-15-216736-6

First edition
H G F E D C B A

The illustrations in this book were done in watercolor and colored pencil, with photographic, digital, and hand-sewn elements, on watercolor paper.
The display type was set in Jacoby.
The text type was set in Meridian.
Color separations by Bright Arts Ltd., Hong Kong
Printed and bound by Tien Wah Press, Singapore
This book was printed on totally chlorine-free Enso Stora Matte paper.
Production supervision by Sandra Grebenar and Ginger Boyer
Designed by Lydia D'moch

You can take off those listening ears and
unzip your lips. I'd better be on my way.

Adios!